Sewing Quilts

by Ann Turner
illustrated by Thomas B. Allen

Macmillan Publishing Company   New York
Maxwell Macmillan Canada   Toronto
Maxwell Macmillan International   New York   Oxford   Singapore   Sydney

First edition
Printed in Hong Kong by South China Printing Company (1988) Ltd.

1   3   5   7   9   10   8   6   4   2
The text of this book is set in 16 pt. Berkeley Old Style Medium.
The illustrations are rendered in pastels on colored paper.
Library of Congress Cataloging-in-Publication Data
Turner, Ann Warren. Sewing quilts / by Ann Turner ; illustrated by Thomas B.
Allen. — 1st ed.   p.   cm. Summary: A pioneer girl sees pieces of her life sewn
into the quilts she, her sister, and her mother make. ISBN 0-02-789285-9
[1. Quilts—Fiction.   2. Quilting—Fiction.   3. Frontier and pioneer life—Fiction.]
I. Allen, Thomas B., ill.   II. Title. PZ7.T8535Se   1994   [E]—dc20   91-4476

For Paula, who cherishes memory
—A. T.

To Hilary Pleasant Allen
—T. B. A.

Mama threads her needle,
holding it up to the light
because her eyes are bad.
Mama says the days are like a quilt,
with small bits and pieces
in between the everything.

And sometimes you can't see
the pattern, Mama says,
until it's all sewn up
and laid upon the bed.

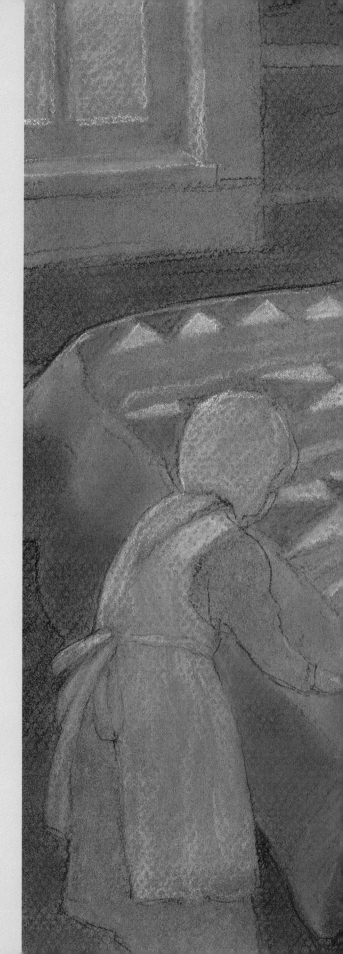

She stitches her School House quilt
with red for the roof, blue for walls
and yellow for the lit windows.
I can almost see the door open
and light spilling onto the snow.

I think when I see Mama's quilt
that it will keep us safe
from fire and loss,
that the snug cloth house
sewn up with tiny stitches
will protect us.
I remember the fire two years back
when flames and smoke
shot out of the roof
and Papa ran and shouted,
getting us out before it was too late.
For days our faces and hands
were raw and red.

Papa built us a new house,
but it's Mama's quilt
that keeps us safe.

Mama starts bean stew,
Mollie sweeps the floor while I
sew by the window.
I piece my Bear Paw quilt,
brown against white.
Once Papa got chased by a bear
and ran so fast he said
his tracks would always be there
in the earth one hundred years from now.
When I stitch the paw down tight
I say inside, Run slow, bear,
catch no one, bear.

Mollie is sewing a doll's quilt
for Clara with the cloth face.
The quilt is red, blue, and white,
and Mollie says it's like our flag.

Mollie was born on Independence Day.
She had a red, wrinkled face and hands,
and little dark eyes like raisins.
"So small for such a long time coming,"
Papa said. That day
I helped him light the Roman candle
and it shot into the sky
like a streak of sun.

When dusk comes,
a piece of dark is caught
in the trees by the creek,
then more and more
until all the red in the sky
is gone.

"Time to stop," Mama says,
and we roll up our sewing
and tuck it away.
Mollie lights the lamp
and sets bean stew on the table.

Papa says a blessing.
Spoons sound against bowls.
The light makes a yellow patch
on the snow outside,
and I wonder if night turns our walls blue,
just like Mama's quilt.

Upstairs, the light is a tiny piece
in the large dark.
Mollie blows it out and we snuggle
under the warm quilt
with the wind calling outside.
Morning, noon, and night
get sewn up in our dreams,

and the next day we start a new line
of blocks, a new bean stew,
a new day.
I will stitch those paws down tight
so no harm can come to Papa,
while Mama sews the house
that keeps us safe.